Animals on the Go

Animals on the Go

Illustrated by Richard Cowdrey

Green Light Readers
Harcourt, Inc.
Orlando   Austin   New York   San Diego   London

Zip! A mouse is little, but it's quick! Animals must be quick to run away from danger and to catch things to eat. Read to find out about some other fast animals.

Wild horses are on the go all the time. If one horse sees danger, it lets the rest know. Then they all run.

An ostrich is too big to fly, but it can run very fast. An ostrich can run just about as fast as a wild horse.

Rabbits are hunted by foxes and bobcats. Rabbits run very fast as they zig and zag through the grass.

If there is danger, a jackrabbit thumps one leg. This lets the rest of the jackrabbits know it's time to run.

Bobcats hunt at night. Even in
the dark, bobcats can see well.

When an animal comes—*zap!*
The bobcat runs fast to catch it.

A cheetah is the fastest animal that lives on land. It can even catch other fast animals.

A cheetah can run as fast as a car, but not for long. In a short time, it has to quit and take a rest.

Look at the map to see some of the
places where these animals live.

ANIMAL MASKS

Make a mask of your favorite animal!

Popsicle stick

crayons or markers

scissors

WHAT YOU'LL NEED

paper plate

colored paper

tape

1. Draw the animal face on a paper plate. Use the colored paper to make ears, whiskers, and a nose.

2. Cut out holes for the eyes.

3. Tape a Popsicle stick to your mask.

4. Wear your mask. Tell a friend what you know about your animal.

Meet the Illustrator

Richard Cowdrey draws pictures for books, calendars, and posters. He lives in a cabin by a pond in the woods. Sometimes he sees animals near his home and draws pictures of them. Which animals do you think Richard Cowdrey has seen around his cabin?

Requests for permission to make copies of any part of the work should be submitted online at www.harcourt.com/contact or mailed to the following address: Permissions Department, Houghton Mifflin Harcourt Publishing Company, 6277 Sea Harbor Drive, Orlando, Florida 32887-6777.

www.HarcourtBooks.com

First Green Light Readers edition 2000
Green Light Readers is a trademark of Harcourt, Inc., registered in the United States of America and/or other jurisdictions.

The Library of Congress has cataloged an earlier edition as follows:
Brett, Jessica.
Animals on the go/Jessica Brett; illustrated by Richard Cowdrey.
p.   cm.
"Green Light Readers."
Summary: Explains that different kinds of animals such as mice, rabbits, and bobcats, need to move fast in order to catch things to eat or to get away from danger.
1. Animals—Miscellanea—Juvenile literature.   2. Animal locomotion—Miscellanea—Juvenile literature.   [1. Animals—Miscellanea.
2. Animal locomotion.]   I. Cowdrey, Richard, ill.   II. Title.
QL49.B738   2000
590—dc21   99-6797
ISBN 978-0-15-204867-9
ISBN 978-0-15-204827-3 (pb)

A C E G H F D B
C E G I J H F D (pb)

Ages 5–7
Grades: 1–2
Guided Reading Level: G–H
Reading Recovery Level: 14–15

Green Light Readers
For the reader who's ready to GO!

"A must-have for any family with a beginning reader."—*Boston Sunday Herald*

"You can't go wrong with adding several copies of these terrific books to your beginning-to-read collection."—*School Library Journal*

"A winner for the beginner."—*Booklist*

Five Tips to Help Your Child Become a Great Reader

1. Get involved. Reading aloud to and with your child is just as important as encouraging your child to read independently.

2. Be curious. Ask questions about what your child is reading.

3. Make reading fun. Allow your child to pick books on subjects that interest her or him.

4. Words are everywhere—not just in books. Practice reading signs, packages, and cereal boxes with your child.

5. Set a good example. Make sure your child sees YOU reading.

Why Green Light Readers Is the Best Series for Your New Reader

● Created exclusively for beginning readers by some of the biggest and brightest names in children's books

● Reinforces the reading skills your child is learning in school

● Encourages children to read—and finish—books by themselves

● Offers extra enrichment through fun, age-appropriate activities unique to each story

● Incorporates characteristics of the Reading Recovery program used by educators

● Developed with Harcourt School Publishers and credentialed educational consultants